Great Explorers

KIT CARSON

Stephen Krensky

A Crabtree Crown Book

Crabtree Publishing
crabtreebooks.com

School-to-Home Support for Caregivers and Teachers

This appealing book is designed to teach students about core subject areas. Students will build upon what they already know about the subject, and engage in topics that they want to learn more about. Here are a few guiding questions to help readers build their comprehensions skills. Possible answers appear here in red.

Before Reading:

What do I know about this topic?

- *I know that Kit Carson was a trapper who explored the Southwest.*
- *I know that Taos, New Mexico is associated with Kit Carson.*

What do I want to learn about this topic?

- *I want to learn more about how Kit Carson was able to survive the difficult journey on the Santa Fe Trail.*
- *I want to learn what type of food Kit and other explorers ate while exploring new parts of America.*

During Reading:

I'm curious to know...

- *I'm curious to know if any women traveled with Kit Carson and the other explorers of the Southwest.*
- *I'm curious to know if the explorers limited their food and water when they crossed the desert.*

How is this like something I already know?

- *I know that some women explored and hunted in the unknown territory of America.*
- *I know that part of the Mojave Desert is called Death Valley and that the temperatures there are usually the hottest in America.*

After Reading:

What was the author trying to teach me?

- *I think the author was trying to teach me about the challenges faced by explorers who were some of the first to travel west.*
- *I think the author was trying to teach me what life was like in the 1800s.*

How did the photographs and captions help me understand more?

- *The picture of the Mojave Desert helped me to understand that the journey was extremely dangerous.*
- *I learned about Kit's journey by looking at the map.*

Table of Contents

Chapter 1: Growing Up

19-year-old Christopher, or Kit, Carson did not think of himself as a "mountain man." It was true that mountain men, or people who lived and worked in the wilderness, spent months trapping beaver and other animals. Kit had done that. It was also  true that mountain men **braved** all kinds of harsh weather hunting in every season. Kit had done that, too. It was even true that mountain men had to fight off wild animals and poisonous snakes they encountered in the wilderness.

And Kit Carson had done that as well.

Despite these similarities, he still didn't think of himself as a mountain man. Not yet. Just a youth himself, he didn't think of himself in the same way as famous mountain men of the time—burly trappers such as Jim Bridger (1804-1881) and Jedidiah Smith (1799-1831).

People had been misjudging Kit by his looks ever since he was a small boy. He was never tall, and according to some, did not have a commanding presence. His father Lindsay, who had fought in the American Revolution before heading to Kentucky to settle down, looked more like

Lindsay Carson

a soldier. Lindsay had five children with his first wife, Lucy. After she died, he had ten more with his second wife, Rebecca. The sixth of these was Kit, born in 1809.

A year later, the Carsons moved to Boone's Lick, Missouri, settling on land bought from the children of the **frontiersman** Daniel Boone. There, Kit grew up in hard times. Everyone's attention on the frontier was focused on growing food and staying alive long enough to eat it. There was little time for fun and games, or even serious pursuits like going to school. Much to his later embarrassment, Kit never learned to read and write.

At 14, Kit was **apprenticed** to a saddle-maker in nearby Franklin. The town was **thriving** because it was the starting point for the Santa Fe Trail, which had opened only a few years earlier. It led from Franklin to the city of Santa Fe, then in northern Mexico.

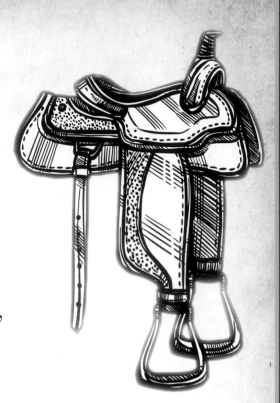

The trail was pioneered by the trader William Becknell following Mexico's successful effort to break free of Spain in 1821. The wandering 900 mile (1,448 km) route followed the Arkansas River into Kansas and then continued southwest. It **grazed** the panhandle of Oklahoma before passing through the Glorieta Mountain Pass and reaching the town of Santa Fe in Mexican territory.

The trail served as the first commercial route across the southwest. Manufactured goods, from sugar and flour to hammers and nails, could now be traded much farther west. The same was true for goods such as furs, wool, and silver traveling the other way.

Santa Fe trail

The lure of the trail drew Kit in a way that the saddle business had not. In August 1826, after only two years into his apprenticeship, Kit abruptly headed west with a group of fur trappers. He didn't know anything about trapping yet, but he took care of the horses and mules and started learning the rest along the way.

As Kit learned more about trapping, he found that he needed to communicate with different people from different backgrounds—both to gather supplies and to sell his furs. Over time, he became fluent in Spanish as well as some **Indigenous** tribal languages.

Chapter 2: Hitting the Trail

When the established trapper Ewing Young asked Kit if he wanted to accompany his expedition from Taos, New Mexico in April of 1829, Kit was ready to go. He joined a crew of 40 men under Young's command. At that time, Taos was under Mexican control. The Mexican government supervised the issuing of trapping **licenses** and deciding who could trap where.

Ewing Young

trap

Not wanting his expedition controlled by the Mexican government, Young let it be known that he was heading north, which he knew would be allowed. But he also planned to turn his men west once they were far enough away from any watchful eyes. There were stories of plentiful beavers and wild horses in California, and Young wanted to find out if they were true.

About fifty miles from Taos, Young turned his party to the southwest. Along the way, the group came across Apache warriors whose people already lived in the area. Young had clashed with the Apache before, on a previous expedition. A **skirmish** followed and although the warriors retreated, they continued to pose a danger as they aimed to defend their **territory**.

Young finally decided to divide the men into two groups. 24 men were sent back to Taos with the furs they had already collected. The remaining 16, including Kit, would continue on to California.

Kit Carson

Chapter 3: Crossing the Desert

The path ahead lay across two deserts, and careful preparations needed to be made. Kit knew how to find water in **barren** country, sometimes from experience and sometimes from his understanding of the landscape. But this knowledge would not always help find water in places where there was no water to be found.

So, the men stitched deerskins together to make sacks that they could fill with water before beginning the trek. Kit later wrote about the land they crossed, describing it as "a country sandy, burned up, and not a drop of water." Men and animals "suffered extremely." But what should they do? Their only choices were to turn back, give up and die, or **trudge** on as best they could.

They decided to trudge on. There were no easy paths to follow. Every step, whether on sand or baked rock, was difficult. They had already crossed 600 miles (966 km) since they had left Taos, and they were close to death from the dangers of the trip.

In fact, they might well have died had they not been helped by local Native Americans. They supplied the group with enough food, such as beans, corn, and horsemeat, to regain their strength and continue their journey.

Native Americans husking and grinding corn

Even so, they still faced almost 300 miles (482 km) of the Mojave Desert. 150,000 years before, this land had been green and comfortable. But times had changed. It now included an area that, about 20 years later, would earn the alarming name of Death Valley.

The Mojave was too big to go around. The only choice was to go through it as quickly as possible. For 13 days, Kit and the rest of Young's party followed the dry bed, or bottom, of the Mojave River. The June heat was **unrelenting**. There was little to eat and even less to drink.

Finally, though, they reached Mission San Gabriel near the site of present-day Pasadena. The mission, founded in 1771, was one of nine California missions established by the Spanish priest Father Junipero Sierra between 1769 and 1782. From these locations with groups of

Father Junipero Sierra

buildings, religious leaders went out to spread the Roman Catholic faith. "They had about eighty thousand head of **stock**," Kit recalled, "fine fields and vineyards—in fact it was a paradise on earth."

Mission San Gabriel today

Everybody who received them at the mission was friendly, which was lucky for Kit and his companions. They were in no condition at that point to defend themselves against anyone.

Chapter 4: More Challenges Ahead

Over the next 10 years, Kit undertook a number of expeditions and hunting trips. In some he was part of large group. In others, he traveled alone, taking his chances in the wilderness. Sometimes he was hungry or cold, and if he became injured, he had to tend to any wounds as best he could on his own.

Perhaps his most frightening moment came in 1834 . While hunting elk, Kit suddenly found himself in the company of two grizzly bears. The bears quickly chased him up a tree. Fortunately, the tree could support his weight—but not the bears'. Unfortunately, the bears were not willing to give up on dinner just yet. So, they shook the tree repeatedly. Kit hugged the trunk as tightly as he could. Finally, the bears gave up and lumbered off. At that moment, Kit remembered, "I was heartily pleased, never having been so scared in my life."

Kit later gained perhaps his greatest fame working as a scout and guide for the explorer John C. Frémont on three expeditions from 1842 to 1845. Each time they went deep into the Oregon territory. Among their goals were to identify the best sites for forts and map out the best areas for settlement.

Kit Carson and John C. Frémont

John Sutter's fort

During his travels, Carson spent the winter of 1844 at John Sutter's fort in northern California, only five years before gold was discovered in the area. He also served in the army during the Mexican War of 1846-1848 and fought for the Union during the Civil War in the 1860s.

In 1858, De Witt C. Peters published a book called *The Life and Adventures of Kit Carson*. The breathless account, supposedly dictated by Carson himself, cemented his fame with the American public. But it was also not above bending the truth and exaggerating some of Carson's deeds. Kit

Kit Carson in 1868

himself was said to have commented that Peters "laid it on [...] too thick."

In Kit Carson's time, the West was largely unexplored by settlers. Traversing the unknown was risky business, but a few men had the bravery and drive to do so. One famous quote from Kit claims that men such as this, "trappers and hunters," were "now almost extinct."

Kit himself, one of the most famous of those trappers and hunters, lived only until 1868. But the memory of his life remains firmly etched in the history of the American frontier.

The grave of Kit Carson in Taos, New Mexico

Glossary

apprenticed: Made an assistant to

barren: Not supporting the growth of plants

braved: Faced a fearful situation

burly: Large, strong, and heavy

frontiersman: A person who lives or works on a frontier, or unsettled area

grazed: Ate grass in a field

Indigenous: Describes the first inhabitants of a place

licenses: Documents granting legal permission to do or own something

skirmish: An irregular and brief fight

stock: A herd of cattle or other farm animals

territory: An area of land controlled by a leader, group, or country

thriving: Doing well, often when growing

trudge: Walk slowly, dragging one's steps

unrelenting: Maintaining strength without pausing

Index

Comprehension Questions

Why was Kit Carson unable to learn to read and write?

What became the name of part of the Mojave Desert?

In which year was the book about Kit Carson's life published?

About the Author

Stephen Krensky is the award-winning author of more than 150 fiction and nonfiction books for children. He and his wife Joan live in Lexington, Massachusetts, and he happily spends as much time as possible with his grown children and not-so-grown grandchildren.

Written by: Stephen Krensky
Designed by: Rhea Wallace
Series Development: James Earley
Proofreader: Janine Deschenes
Educational Consultant: Marie Lemke M.Ed.
Print Coordinator: Katherine Berti

Photo credits: Everett Collection: cover; ehrlif: p. 7; Alex Rockheart: p. 8; LOC: p. 9; Reading Room 2020: p. 11; LOC: p. 12; Viktoriia Bondarenko: p. 13; Science History Images: p. 15; ETgohome: p. 17; Katrina Brown: p. 17; Pictures Now: p. 19; kenkistler: p. 20; LOC: p. 22; Angel DiBilio: p. 23; Martin Rudlof Photography: p. 25; Credit: Science History Images: p. 26; LOC: p. 27; LOC: p. 28; Deborah McCague: p. 29;

Crabtree Publishing

crabtreebooks.com 800-387-7650
Copyright © 2023 Crabtree Publishing

Printed in the U.S.A./012023/CG20220815

Published in Canada
Crabtree Publishing
616 Welland Ave.
St. Catharines, Ontario
L2M 5V6

Published in the United States
Crabtree Publishing
347 Fifth Ave
Suite 1402-145
New York, NY 10016

Library and Archives Canada Cataloguing in Publication
Available at Library and Archives Canada

Library of Congress Cataloging-in-Publication Data
Available at the Library of Congress

Hardcover: 978-1-0398-0013-7
Paperback: 978-1-0398-0072-4
Ebook (pdf): 978-1-0398-0191-2
Epub: 978-1-0398-0131-8